Stratford School Milpitas
341 Great Mall Parkway
Milpitas, CA 95035

The Goblin Princess

Read more
UNICORN DIARIES
books!

Unicorn Diaries

The Goblin Princess

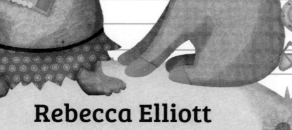

Rebecca Elliott

BRANCHES

SCHOLASTIC INC.

For Frida, my spoilt little puppy princess. —R.E.

Special thanks to Kyle Reed for his contributions to this book.

Copyright © 2020 by Rebecca Elliott

All rights reserved. Published by Scholastic Inc., *Publishers since 1920*. SCHOLASTIC, BRANCHES, and associated logos are trademarks and/or registered trademarks of Scholastic Inc.

The publisher does not have any control over and does not assume any responsibility for author or third-party websites or their content.

No part of this publication may be reproduced, stored in a retrieval system, or transmitted in any form or by any means, electronic, mechanical, photocopying, recording, or otherwise, without written permission of the publisher. For information regarding permission, write to Scholastic Inc., Attention: Permissions Department, 557 Broadway, New York, NY 10012.

This book is a work of fiction. Names, characters, places, and incidents are either the product of the author's imagination or are used fictitiously, and any resemblance to actual persons, living or dead, business establishments, events, or locales is entirely coincidental.

Library of Congress Cataloging-in-Publication Data

Names: Elliott, Rebecca, author, illustrator. | Elliott, Rebecca. Unicorn Diaries ; 4. Title: The goblin princess / Rebecca Elliott. Description: First edition. | New York : Branches/Scholastic, 2020. | Series: Unicorn diaries ; 4 | Summary: Greta the goblin princess is bored, but when unicorns Bo and Sunny try to cheer her up by using their powers to make her queen (for a day), they discover just how much trouble a bored—and spoiled—goblin princess can cause for everyone around her. Identifiers: LCCN 2019059221 | ISBN 9781338323450 (paperback) | ISBN 9781338323467 (library binding) | ISBN 9781338323474 (ebook) Subjects: LCSH: Unicorns—Juvenile fiction. | Goblins—Juvenile fiction. | Magic—Juvenile fiction. | Princesses—Juvenile fiction. | Responsibility—Juvenile fiction. | CYAC: Unicorns—Fiction. | Goblins—Fiction. | Magic—Fiction. | Princesses—Fiction. | Responsibility—Fiction. Classification: LCC PZ7.E45812 Go 2020 | DDC [Fic]—dc23 LC record available at https://lccn.loc.gov/2019059221

10 9 8 7 6 5 4 3 2 1   20 21 22 23 24

Printed in China   62
First edition, December 2020

Edited by Katie Carella
Book design by Marissa Asuncion and Christian Zelaya

Table of Contents

1

Another Magical Week

Sunday

Well, swish my tail, Diary! It's another lovely, sunny week here in Sparklegrove Forest with your favorite unicorn – me!

My name is Rainbow (but you can call me Bo) Tinseltail.

Here's a map of Sparklegrove Forest so you can find your way around.

Rainbow Falls

Troll Caves

Glimmer Glade

Sparklegrove School for Unicorns

Dragon Nests

Budbloom Meadow

Snowbelle Mountain

Unipods

Fairy Village

Twinkleplop
Lagoon

Goblin
Castle

Lots of magical creatures live here . . .

Like goblins! Here are four fun facts about goblins:

Goblins have super strength.

Goblins eat nothing but cupcakes.

Goblins have a queen who lives in Goblin Castle and rules the forest.

The goblin queen has special Goblin Queen Powers. She has the power to fly and she can make others do as she asks. (But she only ever uses these powers for good.)

The goblin queen right now is Queen Juniper. Everyone in the forest loves her! And one day her daughter, the goblin princess, will become queen.

Princess Greta

But enough about goblins. I'm a unicorn!

Horn
Good for scratching.

Body
We glow when we're nervous!

Mouth
Our snoring sounds like music!

Tail
Swishing it makes our Unicorn Power work. It's also useful as a fan in hot weather!

Here are some other **UNIFACTS** for you:

We each have a different Unicorn Power. I'm a Wish Unicorn.

I can grant one wish every week!

When we're happy, the sun shines extra-bright!

We live in **UNIPODS**.

We don't like getting knots in our manes.

I live at Sparklegrove School for Unicorns (S.S.U.) with my friends.

This is my BESTEST friend, Sunny. His power is turning invisible!

Sunny Huckleberry

Crystal-Clear Unicorn

Here are all my friends and our teacher:

Check out their different unicorn powers!

Nutmeg Silvertips

Flying Unicorn

Scarlett Sugarlumps

Thingamabob Unicorn

Jed Glitterock

Weather Unicorn

Monty Dumpling

Size-Changer Unicorn

Piper Forestine

Healer Unicorn

Mr. Rumptwinkle

Shape-Shifter Unicorn

At school, Mr. Rumptwinkle teaches us **GLITTERRIFIC** subjects, like:

UNIBALL SKILLS

STARGAZING

HISTORY OF
SPARKLEGROVE FOREST

MANE AND TAIL
STYLING

Every week, we learn or try to do something new. When we succeed, Mr. Rumptwinkle gives each of us a special unicorn patch! Then we sew it onto our cool patch blankets.

I can't wait to hear what this week's patch will be!

Just Imagine

Monday

Today we all woke up excited to start the week. Before school, we wanted to play together. But we could NOT agree on which game to play.

Let's play uniball!

Let's jump rope instead.

This went on for a LONG time . . . until a small mole started talking to us!

Can't you find a way to all play together?

Mr. Rumptwinkle, is that you?

Of course it is!

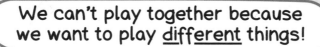

We can't play together because we want to play <u>different</u> things!

Sometimes you just need to use your imagination to solve a problem. What if you make up a <u>new</u> game that makes everyone happy?

We talked about it and came up with the best game ever!

Our new game gave Mr. Rumptwinkle a great idea for this week's patch.

This is the perfect time to work on your IMAGINATION patch!

This week, you will need to use your imaginations to solve problems in the forest.

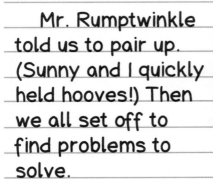

Mr. Rumptwinkle told us to pair up. (Sunny and I quickly held hooves!) Then we all set off to find problems to solve.

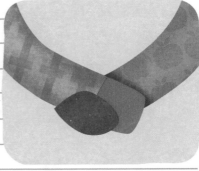

3 A Bad Wish

Sunny and I trotted off to look for any magical creatures who needed help.

You have a great imagination, Bo.

Thanks, Sunny! You too! This week's patch is going to be easy!

18

Then we found not just ANY magical
creature. We found the goblin princess!

I whispered to Sunny.

If we use our imaginations to solve the princess's problem, we can get our patches!

Yes!

Follow us!

We trotted to the tallest tree.

We didn't. So we asked her <u>why</u> she wanted to fly.

I'm stuck in my boring castle all day with no one to play with. If I had magical Goblin Queen Powers, I could fly _and_ make people do what I say. I'd NEVER be bored!

Well, you'll be queen someday.

I want to be queen now! I want to see the forest from above NOW.

Sunny and I looked at each other. We both had the same idea . . .

You could grant Greta a wish to make her queen for a day! Then she could fly!

That's just what I was thinking! AND we used our imaginations. So, we'll get our IMAGINATION patches. Right?

Yes!

We told Greta our idea.

Bo will grant your wish to be queen — but only for ONE day!

Oh, thank you!

Greta made the wish. **SWISH!** A new crown appeared on her head.

Yay! I'm the queen! Now EVERYONE has to do what I say!

Sunny and I realized something that made us worry . . . Sparkles didn't show up like they usually do when we earn patches.

Uh-oh. Maybe we haven't really solved a problem.

Just then, the ACTUAL queen rushed over.

Queen Juniper!

Not anymore — my crown has disappeared! <u>What</u> have you done?

Well, um, Greta was bored and wanted to fly. So we . . . made her the queen.

Just for a day!

Now I'm going to fly back home in case she goes there.

Sorry, but you can't fly today.

Because you're not the queen anymore . . .

Oh, I forgot.

We tried to find Greta for hours, but it was getting late.

Everyone was asleep as Sunny and I climbed onto our cloud beds.

She can't get up to too much trouble overnight. Right, Diary?

The Naughty Queen

Wednesday

This morning our classmates were excited to work on their imagination projects.

Piper and Monty told us about the problem they were trying to fix.

It's Smokey's 300th birthday on Friday! The other dragons want to give him a birthday cake with candles to blow out.

The problem is dragons breathe fire, and he'll set fire to the cake!

Then Scarlett, Jed, and Nutmeg told us about the problem they had found.

The fairies live in mushroom houses. Because it's very hot this summer, the mushrooms need extra water. So the fairies keep having to go get more water.

Their wings are tired from flying to the river so often.

Sunny and I left
before anyone could
ask us how <u>our</u>
project was going!

We galloped around all day looking
for Greta. We couldn't find her anywhere.

But then we saw fireworks in the sky!

But dragons only put on fireworks displays for big royal parties.

ROYAL parties?! I bet the princess has something to do with this!

Follow those fireworks!

We found Piper and Monty near the fireworks. They looked worried.

Just then, Scarlett, Jed, and Nutmeg galloped over. They looked worried, too.

And there's no water left in the river for them to drink, because the dragons drank it all. Now <u>no one</u> has enough water!

Greta has been making animals <u>all over</u> the forest unhappy! She ordered the trolls to juggle rocks. And she made the mermaids do flips — without water!

The whole forest is now one GIANT problem!

I felt AWFUL, and I could tell by Sunny's face that he did, too.

We had to tell our friends what we'd done . . .

Suddenly, the fireworks stopped.

We checked on the forest creatures to make sure they were okay. They were all <u>so</u> tired, they had fallen asleep.

We were tired, too.

I caused so much trouble by granting Greta's wish. But if my friends and I work together, we can fix anything . . . Right?

Fixing the Forest

Thursday

We woke up early. We had a long day ahead of us! We had to find creative ways to help all the forest creatures.

First we visited the trolls. They could hardly lift their arms after juggling rocks for so long.

Monty made himself really big to go talk to them (so they wouldn't try to bully him). Then Piper used her healing power to heal their arms.

Monty and Piper BOTH earned their IMAGINATION patches!

Next, we galloped to Twinkleplop Lagoon, where all of the rivers get their water from. It was empty!

Jed made it rain to fill it up again. Jed earned his patch, too!

TWINKLE-POP!

Thank you!

Then we visited the fairies. They couldn't talk because of their sore throats.

Scarlett used her thingamabob power to magic-up hot honey and lemon for the fairies. She earned her patch!

TWINKLE-POP!

Thank you!

Finally, we visited the dragons.

Nutmeg flew buckets of water up to them. And she earned her patch!

While our friends sang "Happy Birthday" to Smokey, Sunny noticed I looked worried.

Sunny and I went to Goblin Castle.
We found Greta outside.

We sat down next to her.

Back at the **UNIPOD**, we told the others about how Greta was feeling.

We brainstormed ideas.

Then we came up with the best plan ever!

I can't wait for tomorrow!

6
Let's Play!

This morning, my friends and I galloped over to Goblin Castle.

Okay. I'll give it a try.

We played superheroes . . .

Astronauts and aliens . . .

Spies and pirates!

We even played kings and queens so we could ALL pretend we lived in the castle!

Then the ACTUAL queen flew over to us. We bowed.

Thank you all for cheering up my little princess and for helping her see that with great Goblin Queen Power comes great Goblin Queen Responsibility.

Greta, how about I throw you and your new friends a Royal Ball tomorrow?

I have a better idea — let's have an <u>Imagination</u> Ball! That way, we don't need the dragons to breathe fire, or the fairies to sing, or anything else.

That sounds fabulous!

The Imagination Ball

Saturday

Tonight, we had the most **TWINKLE-TASTIC** ball EVER!

We spent the day planning lots of games for the party and trying on our imaginary outfits!

The Imagination Ball was so fun! We
pretended we were at a _very_ fancy party.

We danced to imaginary music and ate imaginary food. Greta even "flew" around pretending to be a fairy!

Greta was SO happy! As we danced, sparkles swirled around Sunny and me! We'd earned our patches!

The party music is delightful!

My <u>Moon Sky Pie</u> is fabulous!

TWINKLE-POP!

TWINKLE-POP!

Then two VERY special guests turned up . . .

Queen Juniper and Mr. Rumptwinkle! They danced together, which made us all giggle.

Finally, it was time for us to collect our patches.

This week, you proved that you have the best, silliest, and most useful imaginations! I'm proud to give out your patches.

Excuse me? Can I have a patch, too?

Well, I'm not sure . . . Are you a <u>unicorn</u>?

That gave me an idea.

Hang on a minute!

I wove a unicorn horn from leaves and handed it to Greta.

Look at me — I'm a unicorn!

Then ALL of us <u>unicorns</u> paraded past Mr. Rumptwinkle (and the queen) to collect our IMAGINATION patches!

We partied until our **HOOVES** couldn't party anymore! I'm SO tired, but I still want to keep partying

I know! I'll party in my dreams! Good night, Diary!

Rebecca Elliott may not have a magical
horn or sneeze glitter, but she's still a lot like a
unicorn. Rebecca always tries to have a positive
attitude, she likes to laugh a lot, and she lives
with some great creatures — her guitar-playing
husband, her noisy-yet-charming children, her
lovable but naughty dog Frida, and a big, lazy
cat called Bernard. She gets to hang out with
these fun characters and write stories for a
living, so she thinks her life is pretty magical!

Rebecca is the author of several picture
books, the young adult novel PRETTY FUNNY,
the Unicorn Diaries early chapter book series,
and the bestselling Owl Diaries series.

Unicorn Diaries

How much do you know about The Goblin Princess?

The unicorns invent uniskip-ball so they can play together. Invent your own game by combining different sports! Using words and pictures, explain how to play your game.

In Chapter 3, Queen Juniper finds out she can no longer fly. Why can't she fly anymore?

Scarlett, Jed, and Nutmeg help the fairies bring water to their houses. Why do the fairies' houses need water? Reread page 34.

Bo brainstorms ways to help Greta. <u>Brainstorm</u> is a compound word, which means that it is made up of other words. What two words make up <u>brainstorm</u>? List as many compound words as you can.

Sunny and Bo teach Greta to use her imagination to have fun. How does your imagination help <u>you</u> have fun? Draw some of the things you like to imagine.